Party!

illustrated by Jess Stockham

Look at the calendar. When is the party?

Let's dress up at the party! Tiger! Giraffe!

Let's make invites. I'll choose the pictures.

You cut them out. Can I stick them on?

This is for you. Please come to my party!

How many more have we got to send?

Everyone will be a different animal.

We'll staple the flags onto the string.

What else do we need? You choose.

Can we get balloons? These have eyes!

This cake mix is hard to stir. My arm aches!

These go in the oven. Put the eyes on!

I'll hang the flags around the room.

We'll play Treasure Hunt. I'll draw the map.

Is everything there? Count the plates!

I want to taste it all! It looks so yummy!

This is my tiger outfit. How do I look?

That was loud! I hope the others don't burst!

Which hat would you like? Mouse or piglet?

Thank you for the card. It looks like me!

Use your hands to feel where the picture is.

Poor elephant! I wonder who will win?

Blow all the candles out! Make a wish!